The Sky Jumps Into Your Shoes At Night

Words and Pictures by Jasper Tomkins

GREEN TIGER PRESS

Published by Simon & Schuster

New York London Toronto Sydney Tokyo Singapore

for the baker in the morning
with the beet on the rise
the bait is on the cliff
and the raccoon points in disguise

The air is the sky.
The wind is the sky.
The blue is the sky.
The sky is a warm blanket
Around our house, the earth.
The sky touches every one of
us in every moment.

This is a book of images
from the life of our dear, happy
friend, the sky.

The sky jumps into your shoes when you take them off at night.

The sky brings you
the smell of flowers in
the morning.

The sky exercises all
the trees.

Little bears like to put their feet in the sky.

The sky likes to squeeze
inside balloons.

The sky can lie upon the
clouds in the warm sun while
you are walking in the rain.

The sky chases itself
around buildings in the city,
just for fun.

Every flower holds a little sky.

The sky holds up all
the rainbows.

The sky is where you look
to think.

The sky waits patiently
inside tunnels for trains to
push it out the other end.

The sky brings you home
from magical journeys.

The sky can sleep in banks
at night where no one else
can go.

The sky would like to push
down every sign.

The sky lies on the waves
and watches the fish.

The sky sets parachutes
gently down to earth.

The sky takes a waterfall
bath when it gets dirty.

The sky sleeps in the
hot desert and dreams
and dreams.

The sky shows you where
it is going.

The sky contains every
word that has ever
been spoken.

The sky picks up old
newspapers so the mountains
can read the news.

The sky makes the ocean dance but leaves your bathtub perfectly calm.

The sky is always ready to play.

The sky lives in seashells
and sings the song of
the ocean.

The sky plants surprise
flower gardens in your yard.

The sky makes your clothes dance when you're not in them.

The sky politely becomes
dark so that you can see our
dear little moon.

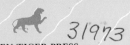

GREEN TIGER PRESS
Simon & Schuster Building, Rockefeller Center, 1230 Avenue of the Americas,
New York, New York 10020.
Copyright © 1986 by Jasper Tomkins.
All rights reserved including the right of reproduction in whole or in part in any form.
GREEN TIGER PRESS is an imprint of Simon & Schuster.
Manufactured in Hong Kong

20   19   18   17   16   15   14   13   12   11

Library of Congress Catalog Card Number 85-082395
ISBN 0-671-74971-4